Philip Roth

The Anatomy Lesson

Vintage International

Vintage Books

A Division of Random House, Inc.

New York

FIRST VINTAGE INTERNATIONAL EDITION, JANUARY 1996

Library of Congress Cataloging-in-Publication Data
Roth, Philip.
The anatomy lesson / Philip Roth. — 1st Vintage International ed.
p. cm.
ISBN 0-679-74902-0
1. Authors, American—Psychology—Fiction. 2. Men authors—Psychology—Fiction. 3. Jewish men—Psychology—Fiction. I. Title.
PS3568.O855A8 1996
813'.54—dc20 95-35202
CIP

Manufactured in the United States of America
10 9 8

The Anatomy Lesson

BOOKS BY Philip Roth

ZUCKERMAN BOOKS

The Ghost Writer
Zuckerman Unbound
The Anatomy Lesson
The Prague Orgy

The Counterlife

American Pastoral
I Married a Communist
The Human Stain

ROTH BOOKS

The Facts
Deception
Patrimony
Operation Shylock

KEPESH BOOKS

The Breast
The Professor of Desire
The Dying Animal

MISCELLANY

Reading Myself and Others
Shop Talk

OTHER BOOKS

Goodbye, Columbus · Letting Go
When She Was Good · Portnoy's Complaint
Our Gang · The Great American Novel
My Life as a Man · Sabbath's Theater

Philip Roth

The Anatomy Lesson

In the 1990s Philip Roth won America's four major literary awards in succession: the National Book Critics Circle Award for *Patrimony* (1991), the PEN/Faulkner Award for *Operation Shylock* (1993), the National Book Award for *Sabbath's Theater* (1995), and the Pulitzer Prize in fiction for *American Pastoral* (1997). He won the Ambassador Book Award of the English-Speaking Union for *I Married a Communist* (1998); in the same year he received the National Medal of Arts at the White House. Previously he won the National Book Critics Circle Award for *The Counterlife* (1986) and the National Book Award for his first book, *Goodbye, Columbus* (1959). In 2000 he published *The Human Stain*, concluding a trilogy that depicts the ideological ethos of postwar America. For *The Human Stain* Roth received his second PEN/Faulkner Award as well as Britain's W. H. Smith Award for the Best Book of the Year. In 2001 he received the highest award of the American Academy of Arts and Letters, the Gold Medal in Fiction, given every six years "for the entire work of the recipient."

VINTAGE

INTERNATIONAL